Solar System Soup

To Jay, for telling me to stop thinking and start writing
and to Scout for always being by my side.

FIRST EDITION

Text Copyright © 2012 by Lindsay Marshall
Illustrations Copyright © 2012 by Don Bearwood

Solar System Soup/ Lindsay Marshall, Don Bearwood —1st ed. pp. 42

ISBN 13: 978-1481250603

Printed in the United States of America.

Solar System Soup

story by **Lindsay Marshall**

Illustrated by **Don Bearwood**

Each year, on Sam's birthday, his Dad would cook him a special meal. Whatever Sam asked for his Dad would make. For his 7th birthday, it was a giant cheeseburger with a stack of pickles three inches high.

When Sam turned 8, he asked for a wedding cake and his Dad delivered.

Last year, Sam ate lobster his Dad had caught himself in the ocean. But this year, just a week away from his 10th birthday, Sam had not decided what to request for his dinner. To be honest, Sam felt a little different about this birthday. He had grown a lot over the past year and felt older. Sam didn't want to hurt his Dad's feelings but he wasn't all that excited about the idea of a special birthday dinner anymore.

That night, while the two were camping under the stars, Sam's Dad asked him what he wanted for his birthday dinner the next week. Sam wanted to tell his Dad that he thought he was getting too old for birthday dinners but he just stayed quiet, acting like he was thinking it over carefully. It then dawned on him that if he asked his Dad for something impossible, something his Dad could never give him, maybe his Dad would understand he was too old for birthday dinners now. He looked up at the stars, thinking it over for real this time, and got an idea.

"Dad", he said, "this year I'm going to ask for the impossible. Something not even you can make me. I would like to have solar system soup." Sam's Dad was quiet as usual and looked up at the sky, a little confused. He should have had questions for Sam, but after a long silence he just said, "Okay son, I'll give it a shot." Sam was surprised his Dad didn't ask him about the ingredients for this strange soup he just thought up a minute before. But since he thought he had made his point about being too old for the birthday dinners, he didn't say anything more.

Sam's Dad loved a challenge and solar system soup was his biggest birthday challenge yet. He woke up in the middle of the night and worked until the sun came up, sketching out his plan for the next seven days. He would have to do all of the preparation work at night so Sam didn't know what he was up to.

The next evening, Sam's Dad set out to collect his first ingredients from the planet Mercury. Since Mercury is the closest planet to the sun, he had to be careful not to get burned collecting ingredients. He used a bow and arrow, tying a special dish under the arrow to collect dust from the planet and a long string to the end of the arrow so he could pull it back once it had landed. That night, while Sam slept, he stood on the roof and used all of his strength to shoot the arrow to Mercury. Using gloves to protect himself from the heat, he pulled back the arrow and collected Mercury's dust. Ingredient number one.

The next night, Sam's Dad set his sights on Venus, the brightest planet in the solar system. Since Venus is closer to Earth than Mercury he figured he could use his trusty boomerang to collect some of its dust. He covered the inside of his boomerang with honey so it could capture some of Venus's dust on its trip. He mustered up his strength and launched the boomerang into the night sky towards Venus, hoping he got the orbit right. Almost an hour later, the boomerang returned with Venus dust attached. Pleased with himself, Sam's Dad called it a night.

The next night it was time to visit Mars, the mystical red planet. Sam's Dad had always wanted to go and figured his trampoline could get him there since Mars is the closest planet to Earth. He jumped off of the roof, onto the trampoline, and then enjoyed the trip to Mars. He only stayed for a few seconds, long enough to collect some dust, before he began the trip home...

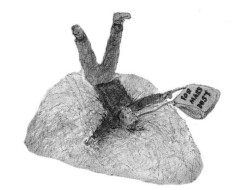

...luckily landing on a stack of hay.

The next morning, over breakfast,

Sam looked at his Dad with curiosity

and asked him if he had heard anything funny the night

before, like a loud crash. His Dad said no and focused on

his breakfast, trying hard to stay awake and not look

suspicious.

That evening, Sam's Dad got ready for his visit to Jupiter, the largest planet in the solar system. He had read a lot about all of Jupiter's moons and decided to take a hot air balloon so he could enjoy a more leisurely trip and take it all in. When he was sure Sam was asleep, he fired up the hot air balloon and took flight towards Jupiter. The trip took all night but it was his most relaxing journey yet. When he got home, he was a little sad Sam hadn't enjoyed the trip with him.

The next night Sam's Dad visited Saturn with its beautiful rings. He rigged up his bicycle with wings and rode nearly all night to get there, collecting dust off of one of its rings before returning home.

The next morning, Sam's Dad woke up and realized he had three planets left to visit in just one night. The next day was Sam's birthday and he would need the whole day to cook the soup. He came up with a plan to gather the ingredients from all three planets in just one trip. Standing on his roof that night, he caught a ride with a passing hawk to the nearest comet, and then rode all the way to Pluto, passing Uranus and Neptune on the way.

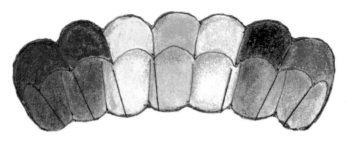

He jumped off at dawn near home, using a parachute to land safely. That night Sam's Dad slept soundly knowing he had all the ingredients he needed for the soup.

The next day was Sam's 10th birthday and after opening his presents in the morning he headed off to school. He didn't like having to go to school on his birthday but he enjoyed the cupcakes at lunch. Riding home that afternoon on the bus, he wondered what his Dad had decided to make him. He started to get excited and was feeling badly that he had thought he was too old for birthday dinners. At the same time, Sam's Dad was putting the finishing touches on his pot of soup and was trying to shake off his yawns.

33

When Sam arrived home his Dad greeted him with a big "Happy Birthday!" and unveiled a huge pot of steaming soup. "Here you are son, you're very own solar system soup!" his Dad said. Sam tried the soup and had never tasted anything like it before. It tasted out of this world! He told his Dad how much he loved it and asked what he put in it. "Well I put the solar system in it, son" his Dad explained, "a little bit from each planet, and some salt and pepper." Sam didn't know what was in the soup but he didn't care it was so delicious. He ate every last drop.

When they were finished with dinner Sam thanked his Dad, who was starting to nod off at the table. He went upstairs to brush his teeth and on his way back to his room he noticed that his Dad's study door was open with all kinds of strange things inside he had never seen before like a bike with wings, a folded up trampoline, and a hot air balloon basket.

The warm soup helped Sam sleep soundly. And that night he dreamt about visiting all of the planets in the solar system with his Dad, using those strange things he had seen in his study.

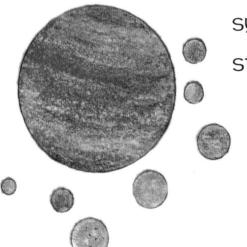

ABOUT THE AUTHOR

Lindsay Marshall is an attorney and director of
the Florence Immigrant & Refugee Rights Project,
an organization that provides free legal services
to immigrants detained in Arizona for deportation
proceedings. She loves to read and write
stories in her free time; taking inspiration from
nature, animals, and things she can't analyze or
understand. She lives in Tucson, Arizona.

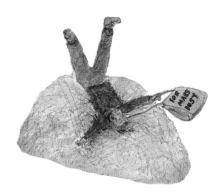

ABOUT THE ILLUSTRATOR

Don Bearwood, a native of Seattle Washington has enjoyed drawing from a very early age, enhancing his talent with studies at the University of Washington. He owned a lighting manufacturing company where he designed and built chandeliers for hotels, churches, etc. up and down the west coast. In retirement he spends his time between Washington State and Arizona doing renderings of historic places.

19811905R00023

Made in the USA
Lexington, KY
07 January 2013